This book belongs to

Brian the Lion
Goes into Space

Tracey Radford

CICO **kidz**

Brian the Lion loved staring at stars,
and dreamt of adventures
on planets like Mars.
For that was where he longed to be,
way up there in the galaxy.

It had to be more fun than here,
to Brian that seemed very clear,
as life on the plain was terribly boring,
with the lying around and endless snoring...

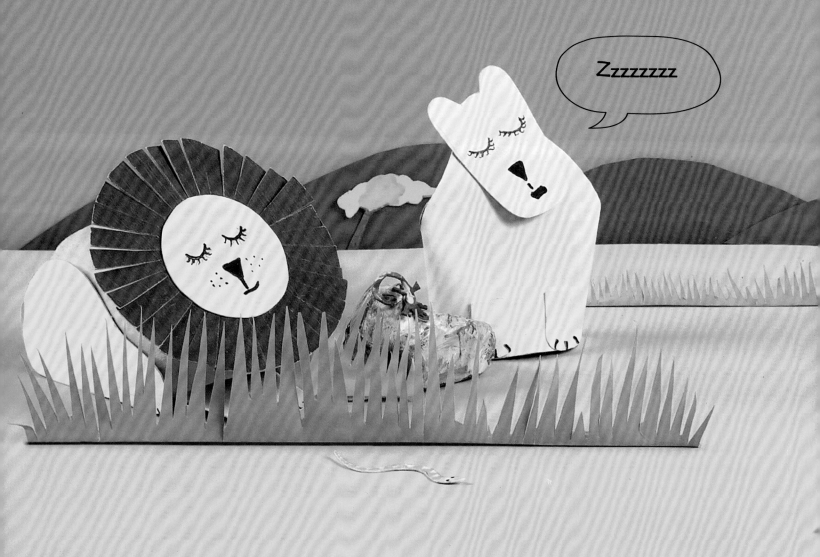

He talked about going to space no end
and drove the others round the bend.
So they bought him a kit with all he'd need
to build a rocket that flew at high speed.

Brian couldn't believe his eyes,
it had to be the BEST surprise!

Phew, he's happy

He started on it straight away
and didn't stop for food all day.

(Luckily, the instructions were simple to follow
and all the tools were easy to borrow.)

Before you could say "Lions in Space!"
the rocket was ready and all was in place.
Brian's friends came to say goodbye
and he blasted off into the sky.

Soon it went pitch black outside,
so Brian sat back for the ride.
He zoomed past the Moon and Mercury
and looped the loop while sipping tea.

Then after he'd made an
interesting pattern,
Brian landed the rocket on
a moon near Saturn.

He ate a snack then ventured out
and almost choked, for all about
were beards with hats, or more precisely
small blue gnomes who spoke quite nicely.

But their words all sounded odd,
so he just smiled and gave a nod.

They made him soup and rainbow bread,
then used pink grass to make his bed.

And after everyone was fed,
the gnomes slept standing on their heads!

Brian was finding it hard to sleep,
so he counted beards instead of sheep...

The gnomes were thrilled to have a guest
and showed him places they liked best—
the purple fort, the orange forest
(home to their pet dragon, Norris).

Each day brought a new surprise,
like flying books and moon-beam pies,
or making gems from fresh dew drops,
the gnomes just never seemed to stop!

Brian could barely stay awake,
so sometimes hid to have a break...

He lost his smile as the weeks went by
and it wasn't hard to work out why.

Brian missed his pride,
he missed just playing,
he missed understanding what
others were saying!

Now when he gazed at the twinkly night sky,
with stars and meteors shooting by,
a space adventure didn't come close
to being with those he loved the most.

So he bid farewell to the busy gnomes
and set a course for planet home.
Norris helped him on his way
by lighting up the engine bay.

Brian touched down at half past three,
just after nap-time, thankfully.

All the lions gathered round
and no one made a single sound,
as Brian told them where he'd been
and who he'd met and what he'd seen.

Gnomes... and dragons...
and flying books!

Soon life slowed down to its normal pace,
which suited Brian in any case,
as now it didn't seem so boring,
he didn't even mind the snoring.

He still gazed at the stars and
thought about things,
like how many feathers he'd need
to make wings...

Brian would never stop
dreaming, you see,
but for now he was just where
he wanted to be.

Make Your Own Brian the Lion

Step-by-step instructions on how to make Brian, and lots of other animals, can be found in Tracey Radford's book *Make Your Own Zoo*, and at her website www.patchworkparent.blogspot.co.uk.

Everything in this book is made by Tracey, mostly from ordinary bits and pieces that are usually recycled or thrown away—see what you can spot!

Published in 2018 by CICO Books
An imprint of Ryland Peters & Small Ltd
20–21 Jockey's Fields   341 E 116th St
London WC1R 4BW   New York, NY 10029

www.rylandpeters.com

10 9 8 7 6 5 4 3 2 1

ISBN: 978 1 78249 576 5

Printed in China

Editor: Dawn Bates
Designer: Eliana Holder
Photographer: Martin Norris
Art director: Sally Powell
Production controller: Mai-Ling Collyer
Publishing manager: Penny Craig
Publisher: Cindy Richards